A Quiet Girl

A Quiet Girl

Peter Carnavas

pajamapress

First published in Canada and the United States in 2020

Text and illustration copyright © 2019 Peter Carnavas
This edition copyright © 2020 Pajama Press Inc.
First published in Australia in 2019 by University of Queensland Press, PO Box 6042, St. Lucia, Queensland 4067 Australia

10 9 8 7 6 5 4 3 2 1

www.pajamapress.ca   info@pajamapress.ca

ONTARIO ARTS COUNCIL
CONSEIL DES ARTS DE L'ONTARIO
an Ontario government agency
un organisme du gouvernement de l'Ontario

Canadä

The publisher gratefully acknowledges the support of the Canada Council for the Arts and the Ontario Arts Council for its publishing program. We acknowledge the financial support of the Government of Canada through the Canada Book Fund (CBF) for our publishing activities.

Library and Archives Canada Cataloguing in Publication

Title: A quiet girl / Peter Carnavas.
Names: Carnavas, Peter, 1980- author, illustrator.
Description: Originally published: St. Lucia, Queensland : University of Queensland Press, 2019.
Identifiers: Canadiana 20190229071 | ISBN 9781772781229 (hardcover)
Classification: LCC PZ7.C268 Qu 2020 | DDC j823/.92—dc23

Publisher Cataloging-in-Publication Data (U.S.)

Names: Carnavas, Peter, author, illustrator.
Title: A Quiet Girl / Peter Carnavas.
Description: Toronto, Ontario Canada : Pajama Press, 2020. | Originally published by University of Queensland Press, Australia, 2019. | Summary: "Mary, a young girl with a meditative disposition, finds her quiet curiosity at odds with her boisterous family. Eventually, Mary is so still that she seems to fade from her family's sight. When calling loudly for her gets no result, the family tries quiet waiting instead and find both Mary and the simple beauty in slowing down to listen to the world"— Provided by publisher.
Identifiers: ISBN 978-1-77278-122-9 (hardback)
Subjects: LCSH: Families -- Juvenile fiction. | Individual differences -- Juvenile fiction. | Quietude – Juvenile fiction. | BISAC: JUVENILE FICTION / Visionary & Metaphysical. | JUVENILE FICTION / Social Themes / Emotions & Feelings.
Classification: LCC PZ7.C376Qui |DDC [F] – dc23

Original art created with ink and watercolor
Cover and text—based on original design by Jo Hunt

Manufactured in China by WKT Company

Pajama Press Inc.
181 Carlaw Ave. Suite 251 Toronto, Ontario Canada, M4M 2S1

Distributed in Canada by UTP Distribution
5201 Dufferin Street Toronto, Ontario Canada, M3H 5T8

Distributed in the U.S. by Ingram Publisher Services
1 Ingram Blvd. La Vergne, TN 37086, USA

For Kaz

Mary was a quiet girl.

She thought quiet thoughts,

stepped quiet steps,

and whispered quiet words.

ZZZZZZZ

Because Mary was quiet,
she heard things nobody else heard.

A dragonfly buzzing through the air.

The soft sigh of the sleeping dog
next door.

The gentle creak of the tree
at the end of her street.

Mary had always been quiet,
but there was just one problem.

Nobody could hear her.

So Mary tried to speak up...

but it was still not loud enough.

So Mary decided to be quieter
than she had ever been before.

Suddenly, the world unfolded
around Mary as her senses were filled
with more beautiful things.

A leaf hanging from a fine
thread of spider silk.

The smell of freshly cut grass.

The tickle of the breeze
ruffling her hair.

Now that Mary was very quiet,
her family hardly noticed her at all.

Soon she became so quiet

she felt like she just wasn't there.

At first, nobody missed Mary.

Then a small gray bird
appeared at the window.

"Mary," said Mom.
"Is this the bird you were...?"

"Mary?
Where *is* Mary?"

"MARY!"

called Mom.

Their calls grew louder and louder

until the whole neighborhood echoed
with the sound of Mary's name.

Finally, Mom and Dad stopped calling.
They fell silent and listened.

Wind chimes clinked in the breeze.

Bees hummed as they danced in the clover.

And then, at last,
the most marvelous sound of all...

Mary's voice, singing a small song.

♫ La la ♪
de da

"Mary," said Mom.
"Have you been here the whole time?"

"Yes," whispered Mary.

"But we didn't hear you," said Dad, "until we were..."

"Quiet," said Mary.

They didn't ask her to speak up
or use a nice, loud voice.

Instead, they sat beside her
and listened for all of the small wonderful things
that lay hidden in the world.

Mindfulness: Feeling Quiet Inside

Mindfulness is a way of helping our minds and bodies by taking the time to be still and pay attention. Like Mary's family, we can feel calmer, more focused, and even happier when we are quiet and notice everything that is happening in and around us.

Ways to be mindful:

1. Sit quietly and breathe in and out. Pay attention to the way your tummy moves with every breath. You can place a hand on your tummy to help you feel it.

2. Go outside and stand or sit very still. Notice one thing that you can see, one thing that you can smell, one thing that you can hear, and one thing that you can feel.

3. Choose a place to sit in a park or school yard. See how many insects, birds, and other critters you can spot without moving.

4. Take a walk with your family. Point out everything you see that you have never noticed before.

5. Close your eyes and listen. What is the quietest sound you can hear?

Peter Carnavas' career as a primary school teacher inspired him to embrace his passion for children's literature. His picture book *Blue Whale Blues* won the Society of Children's Book Writers and Illustrators Crystal Kite Award, and *My Sister is a Superhero* won an Australian Book Industry Award. *The Elephant*, Peter's first novel, won the Children's Book Award at the Queensland Literary Awards. He lives on Australia's Sunshine Coast with his family.